TRACTOR MAC
FARMERS' MARKET

Written and illustrated by

BILLY STEERS

FARRAR STRAUS GIROUX · NEW YORK

"**S**OMEONE ATE MY PIECE of birthday cake," said Carla the chicken one sunny morning on Stony Meadow Farm. "I was saving it as a treat for when it got nice and stale," she clucked.

"Hmmm," said Tractor Mac.

"Somebody got into the garbage cans, and it wasn't me!" cried Goat Walter.

"Ahh," said Tractor Mac.

"Something raided the pantry," meowed Pepper the cat. "It ate all the sugar and lard!"

"I see," said Tractor Mac with a sigh. "I think I know who is behind all of this. Let's pay a visit to our friends Pete and Paul."

They found Pete and his brother Paul in their pen.

"Yuck! What is that smell?" said Carla.

"Just stuff we found," replied Pete.

"Eating is our favorite hobby," grunted Paul happily.

"Eating and snacking," agreed Pete.

"Do you even know what you're eating?" asked Tractor Mac.

"Uhh . . . something brown, I think," answered Paul.

"If you like food, you'll like the farmers' market," said the big red tractor. "Farmer Bill is bringing you with us today. There's loads of freshly made goods and locally grown food."

"Better than what you're eating right now," added Carla.

"Food?" asked Pete.

"Like at the fair?" asked Paul. "I love fair food! French fries, fried dough, fried onions, fried anything! Cotton candy, ice cream, salted pretzels, fudge brownies, and soda pop! Fair food is *great* food!"

"Fair food is not always great food," corrected Tractor Mac.

"He's right, Paul," said Pete. "Remember what happened last year at the fair when you ate all that junk food?"

"Oh yeah," said Paul with a sigh. "I felt awful for a week! I don't ever want to feel that way again!"

When they got to the farmers' market it was busy as usual.

"Wow!" exclaimed Paul.

"All the neighboring farmers and growers are here," said Pete.

Booths were filled with fruits, vegetables, nuts, and seeds. Tables held milk and cheese, eggs and honey.

FARMERS' MARKET

CORN

Melons

Flowers

Fruit

Crafts

Veggies

Plants

FRESH!

LOCAL GROW

PET A PIG

Tucker Pickup tooted his horn. "Machines like Tractor Mac and me need fresh gas and new oil regularly to keep us running smoothly."

"The fresh food you'll find here will keep you healthy and strong," added Tractor Mac.

"Mmm . . . that's a good smell!" said Pete. "There are many different and healthy ways to prepare food," said Tractor Mac. "You can grill, bake or broil, sauté or steam."

"I like mine raw!" cheered Paul.

The next day the animals at Stony Meadow Farm
were excited. The day after a farmers' market
meant good food for all.

"Hey! Someone took my melon,"
said Carla.

"Somebody got into the vegetables!"
cried Goat Walter. "And it wasn't me!"

"Something raided the pantry
again," meowed Pepper the cat.
"But only the bowls are missing."

"We thought we'd put out a 'locally grown' spread for all of us," said Pete with a laugh.

"Snacks and sweets are okay for a treat, but real food is *great* food!" said Paul.

"Eating fresh and mostly green will keep you healthy and keep you lean," said Tractor Mac with a big grin.

FAVORITE RECIPES
For Kids and Adults

COOKING FRESH FOOD CAN BE A LOT OF FUN. ASK AN ADULT IF YOU CAN HELP MAKE THESE HEALTHY DISHES.

BASIL PESTO

1 cup packed basil
3 tablespoons roasted pine nuts
3 garlic cloves
Salt to taste
Olive oil

Roast pine nuts in a preheated 350° F. oven for 5–7 minutes or until lightly golden. Place garlic cloves with skins on in a small saucepan, cover cloves with olive oil, and cook on low heat until skins start to color and insides feel soft. Remove skin from cloves.

Place basil, pine nuts, and garlic in a food processor and pulse to combine (or use a mortar and pestle). Drizzle olive oil from the garlic pan, and process until everything is thoroughly mixed. Taste and add salt if needed.

When finished, cover pesto directly with plastic wrap so it does not darken. Enjoy with pasta, pan-seared scallops, or your favorite vegetable.

SAUTÉED KALE

1 bunch kale
1–2 garlic cloves
Salt and pepper
Extra virgin olive oil

Place kale in a bowl of water and let dirt settle to the bottom. Lift kale out of the bowl, pat dry, and gently tear off the rib. Roughly chop the leaves to equal small bites. Peel, then mince or thinly slice the garlic and set aside. Bring a pot of water to a boil, then salt generously. Place kale in boiling water for 1 minute, and then drain. Heat a sauté pan over medium high heat. Drizzle olive oil in the pan, add garlic, and quick sauté until fragrant. Place kale in pan, and sauté until cooked. Season with salt and pepper.

CONNECTICUT BLUEBERRY MUFFINS

2½ cups plus 1 tablespoon flour

2 teaspoons baking powder

1 teaspoon baking soda

½ teaspoon salt

½ cup light brown sugar, packed

2 farm eggs, lightly beaten

1⅓ cups fresh milk,
    at room temperature

½ cup melted unsalted butter

1½ teaspoons vanilla extract

1½ cups blueberries

1 teaspoon lemon zest

Preheat oven to 375° F. Butter muffin tin. Mix 2 cups flour, baking powder, baking soda, salt, and brown sugar together. In a separate bowl, mix eggs, milk, melted butter, and vanilla extract. In a third bowl, toss fresh blueberries with lemon zest and one tablespoon flour. Combine the egg and flour mixtures until just blended, then add the blueberry mixture. Scoop batter into muffin tin, and place in upper third of oven. Bake until brown and well risen, about 25 minutes. Makes 9–12 muffins.

APPLESAUCE

3 pounds apples, peeled and quartered

Fresh lemon juice

Local honey (optional)

Cinnamon or allspice or cardamom
    (optional)

Place peeled and quartered apples in pot on stove with water (about ¼ cup), cover, and cook until apples are tender. Sweeten with honey, lemon, and spices to taste. Simmer for about 5 minutes. Mash a little more with fork and let cool. Enjoy.

FACTS FOR KIDS
—— To Tell Their Parents ——

FRUITS AND VEGETABLES come in many different colors, and each one has a different job in keeping your body in tip-top shape. Eat a rainbow of them to be at your healthiest.

WHOLE-GRAIN FOODS ARE made from the nutritious part of the grain. Foods made from refined grains—such as white bread—are not. Eat mostly whole grains to give you lasting energy.

IT IS IMPORTANT TO EAT a healthy breakfast every day. It gets your brain and body started for a full day of learning and playing.

FOODS THAT ARE GROWN on farms near where you live are fresh, tasty, and healthful. You can buy them at the farmers' market or take your mom and dad to the farm and pick your own.

EATING FRESH WHOLE FOODS, exercising, and playing outside in the sunshine help your heart, muscles, and bones grow healthy and strong.

This book is dedicated to stewards of the land and sea and tillers of the soil, past, present, and future. Thanks to Anne Gallagher, Dr. Hack, Dr. D'Isidori, and Marydale Debor.

Farrar Straus Giroux Books for Young Readers
175 Fifth Avenue, New York 10010

Copyright © 2009 by Billy Steers
All rights reserved
Color separations by Bright Arts (H.K.) Ltd.
Printed in China by Toppan Leefung Printing Ltd.,
Dongguan City, Guangdong Province
Designed by Kristie Radwilowicz
Previous edition published by Tractor Mac, LLC
First Farrar Straus Giroux edition, 2015
3   5   7   9   10   8   6   4   2

mackids.com

Library of Congress Cataloging-in-Publication Data
Steers, Billy, author, illustrator.
    Tractor Mac: farmers' market / Billy Steers. — First Farrar Straus Giroux edition.
        pages cm
    Originally published in Roxbury, Connecticut, by Tractor Mac in 2009.
    ISBN 978-0-374-30107-1 (paper over board)
    [1. Tractors—Fiction.   2. Pigs—Fiction.   3. Food—Fiction.   4. Food habits—Fiction.
5. Farm life—Fiction.]   I. Title.   II. Title: Farmers' Market.

PZ7.S81536Tqs 2015
[E]—dc23
                                                                                        2014043838

Farrar Straus Giroux Books for Young Readers may be purchased for business or promotional
use. For information on bulk purchases please contact Macmillan Corporate and Premium
Sales Department at (800) 221-7945 x5442 or by email at specialmarkets@macmillan.com.

ABOUT THE AUTHOR

Billy Steers is an author, illustrator, and commercial pilot. In addition to the Tractor Mac series, he has worked on forty other children's books. Mr. Steers had horses and sheep on the farm where he grew up in Connecticut. Married with three sons, he still lives in Connecticut. Learn more about the Tractor Mac books at www.tractormac.com.